SALT HANDS

by Jane Chelsea Aragon

illustrated by
Ted Rand

E. P. DUTTON · NEW YORK

Text copyright © 1989 by Jane Chelsea Aragon
Illustrations copyright © 1989 by Ted Rand

Library of Congress Cataloging-in-Publication Data

Aragon, Jane Chelsea.
    Salt hands/by Jane Chelsea Aragon; illustrated by Ted Rand.
        p.   cm.
    Summary: In the middle of the night a young girl wakens
to a sound, goes outdoors, discovers a deer with whom she sits
quietly and lets him lick salt she has sprinkled on her hands.
    ISBN 0-525-44489-0
    [1. Deer—Fiction.   2. Night—Fiction.]   I. Rand, Ted, ill.
II. Title.   88-38470
PZ7.A66Sal   1989   CIP
[E]—dc19   AC

Published in the United States by
E. P. Dutton, New York, N.Y.,
a division of NAL Penguin Inc.

Published simultaneously in Canada by
Fitzhenry & Whiteside Limited, Toronto

Designer: Barbara Powderly

Printed in Hong Kong by South China Printing Co.
First Edition   10 9 8 7 6 5 4 3 2 1

to my brother,
Lawrence David Birnbaum
J.C.A.

to Billie Barner
T.R.

In the night
I woke up.

I heard something outside
like a rustle
or a breath.

There was a deer under the pear tree.
The moon cast a shadow
of his antlers on the ground.

I went to the door.
It was dark.
It was still.
The night air was warm.

I didn't want to frighten the deer,
so quietly
I went in
and sprinkled some salt into my hands.

I tiptoed outside
and stepped toward him
silently.
He looked at me.
His eyes were big and brown.
He watched me for a long time.

I knelt on the grass.
The deer flicked his white tail
back and forth.
I sang a song to him
softly,
while he nibbled on fallen pears.

He shook his head
and twitched his ears.
He was listening to my song.

He moved closer to me
cautiously.
I whispered my song.
Then slowly,
I held out my hands.

My heart beat quickly
as I sat as still as the grass,
as still as the night.
I didn't want him to run away.

There was not a sound
as he came near me.
He came very close.

As I looked up at him,
I could see into his eyes.
They were gentle,
and I knew he was not afraid.

He lowered his head
calmly
and sniffed my hands.
Then he tasted the salt.

For a moment
I held my breath.
I didn't move.
His whiskers tickled my fingers.
I kept my palms still.

He licked my hands
until the salt was all gone.

When he was finished,
he raised his head and turned away
slowly
and walked off into the night.